# SAM'S BIG DEER

Written by James Stearns ★ Illustrations by Jason King

Sam stretched and yawned while waking up on this sunny Saturday morning. He was immediately pounced upon by the best dog ever, Pepper. Dad had gone deer hunting and they had the whole day to play.

Sam didn't get to go hunting because it was too far to hike and Sam was still too small. But, Sam thought, "I can find a deer," – and that was just what he planned to do.

Sam packed hunting gear neatly into a backpack, just like Dad, as Pepper eagerly tried to help. "Pep, we are going to find a deer today," Sam proclaimed.

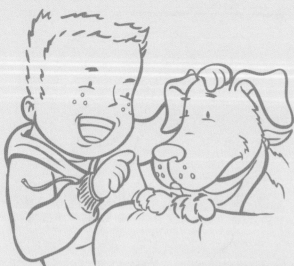

"Pep, this is a big hunting adventure, and you will have to be strong and hike a long way," Sam explained. Pep licked Sam's face to say, "Yep, I am ready to go," and off into the wilderness Sam and Pep went.

It was not long until Pep froze in his tracks as Sam looked ahead. "That's a rabbit, silly dog. We are looking for deer, and some of them have antlers, don't you know?" Sam told Pep.

After a little thought, Sam decided they should chase the rabbit for practice, "Go get him," Sam shouted to Pep, and the chase was on.

"That was close, Pep, but I think the rabbit got away,"
Sam said as they hiked deeper into the woods.

"Hey Pep, I think I see a deer over there behind that old log. I can see some fur," Sam described. As Sam and Pep tip-toed around to peek at what was behind the log, they came face to face with A BEAR!!!

Sam wanted to scream and run, but instead he held on to Pep with shaking legs and slowly walked backwards until they could no longer see the bear.

Sam and Pep then ran until they could barely breathe. "This is a pretty dangerous hunt, Pep. We need to be more careful," Sam insisted.

After all the excitement, Sam and Pep were starting to feel hungry! Sitting down on a log, Sam pulled some tasty snacks out of the backpack to share with Pep.

Sam was feeling a little sleepy when the snap of a stick grabbed their attention. "Pep, don't move. I see a deer with big antlers," Sam whispered with big eyes.

Sam slid down behind the log and pointed the rifle at the big buck. As the buck stepped out into the open, Sam let out a loud shout, "KaPow!"

"Pep, now that's how you get a deer! You and I might just be the best hunters in the woods!" Sam exclaimed. Pep agreed and began licking the lucky hunter's face with his tail a-wagging.

It was now getting late. Sam and Pep began the long hike back home through the woods.

As Sam marched into the warm house, that familiar voice called from the kitchen. "What did you do today?" Sam's mother asked.

"Oh, not much. Pep and I probably only got the biggest deer in the woods! Maybe next time I can go along to show dad how to get a really big deer," Sam replied.

**JAMES ★ STEARNS**

Growing up in Montana provided me with a deep love and appreciation of the outdoors, along with the wild things that inhabit them. My writings are a dedication to never losing our childhood sense of adventure, as well as providing our children of today with stories that inspire the imagination to dream about adventures of their own.

**JASON ★ KING**

Jason King is an illustrator and graphic designer who loves to make big stories come to life. From his home nestled in the heart of the West, he creates visual worlds filled with an honest sense of fun and adventure, with a bit of old-school flair.

ISBN 13: 978-1-59152-163-1

Published by JSM INC

© 2015 by James Stearns

For more information, write: JSM Inc. - P.O. Box 2016 - Bozeman, MT. 59771
To see more Jason King illustration visit: www.heymisterking.com

You may order extra copies of this book by calling Farcountry Press toll free at (800) 821-3874.

Produced by Sweetgrass Books.
PO Box 5630, Helena, MT 59604; (800) 821-3874; www.sweetgrassbooks.com.

Printed in the United States of America.

19   18   17   16   15          1   2   3   4   5